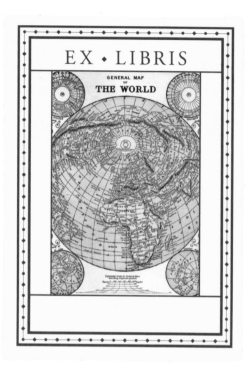

EX · LIBRIS

GENERAL MAP
OF
THE WORLD

A catalogue record for this book is available
from the British Library

Published by Ladybird Books Ltd
A subsidiary of the Penguin Group
A Pearson Company

LADYBIRD and the device of a Ladybird are trademarks of
Ladybird Books Ltd Loughborough Leicestershire UK

© Disney MCMXCIV

Dìsney

THE LITTLE MERMAID

Ladybird

Down in the deepest ocean, there once lived a mermaid princess called Ariel. She was the youngest daughter of King Triton, ruler of the merpeople, and she had the most beautiful singing voice in the whole of his kingdom. Her father loved her dearly, but she was always getting into trouble.

Ariel longed to be part of the human world and spent her time exploring old shipwrecks. The Sea-King feared for her safety and, thinking humans were dangerous, warned her to stay away from them. But the little mermaid was certain he was wrong.

When Ariel was sixteen years old, King Triton arranged for her to sing in a magnificent concert, and merpeople came from all over the kingdom to hear her.

That evening Ariel was so busy exploring with her friend Flounder that she forgot all about the concert! She had found some human treasures and taken them to the surface to ask Scuttle the seagull what they were.

King Triton was furious. "You could have been seen by one of those humans!" he raged. "I'm never to hear of you going to the surface again. Is that clear?"

Ariel tried to protest but her father wouldn't listen. He ordered Sebastian, Ariel's music teacher, to keep an eye on her. But it wasn't an easy task!

One night Sebastian followed Ariel and Flounder to the surface to watch a ship! On board the crew were celebrating the birthday of a handsome young prince called Eric, and Ariel watched them in delight.

Soon storm clouds gathered overhead.
Huge waves wrecked the ship and Eric
was flung into the sea. Ariel swam quickly
to his rescue and pulled him towards the
shore.

"Look! He's breathing!" cried Ariel. She gazed at Eric and fell deeply in love. Then, as she sang to him, his eyes began to open. But, hearing a voice in the distance, Ariel slipped back into the water and hid behind a nearby rock. She watched as Eric's servant led him away.

When they were out of sight, Ariel swam home. "Some day," she vowed to herself, "I'm going to be part of that human world."

Sebastian had seen everything, and it was not long before the Sea-King learnt that Ariel was in love with a human. Triton was very angry. Determined to teach his daughter a lesson, he stormed into her secret grotto and destroyed all her beloved human treasures.

Heartbroken, Ariel sat down and wept. Above her two sly-looking eels called Flotsam and Jetsam emerged from the shadows. The little mermaid looked up.

"Poor sweet child," they hissed. "Don't be scared. We know someone who can make all your dreams come true. Ursula has great powers."

"The Sea-Witch!" gasped Ariel. She knew that Ursula was her father's worst enemy, who had been banished from his kingdom many years ago and who was now seeking revenge.

Ariel hesitated. Then, thinking that it was her only chance to win Prince Eric's love, the little mermaid swam away with the evil eels – quickly followed by Flounder and Sebastian.

Ursula greeted Ariel gleefully. "The only way to get what you want," the Sea-Witch explained, "is to become human yourself. And fortunately I know a little magic.

"Now listen, here's the deal. In exchange for your voice, I will turn you into a human for three days. If Eric hasn't given you the kiss of true love in that time, you will become a mermaid again and belong to me for ever."

A scroll appeared in Ursula's hand. "Go ahead and sign," she urged.

Ariel was terrified but, thinking of Eric again, she signed. A moment later she was walking on the seashore – a human at last!

hereby grant unto Ursula the Witch of the Sea... one voice.

eternity

Prince Eric had been searching everywhere for the girl with the beautiful voice who had rescued him. He had almost given up hope of finding her, when he noticed someone sitting on a rock. This girl looked familiar, but when he found she couldn't speak, Eric realised sadly that she was not the one.

Feeling sorry for the voiceless girl, he
led her back to the palace. And the next
day, Eric took Ariel on a tour of his
kingdom. They enjoyed being together
and Ariel was sure the Prince was falling in
love with her.

Later that afternoon, when they were
boating on a lake, Eric bent forward to
kiss Ariel – but at that very moment the
boat was overturned.

The Sea-Witch had been watching
them, and fearing her plan was about to
fail, she had sent her precious eels to take
action. Now disguised as Vanessa, a
beautiful maiden, and with Ariel's voice
trapped in a seashell necklace, Ursula
made her way to the shore, where the
Prince was wandering alone.

As soon as Eric heard Ariel's voice he was entranced, and fell completely under its spell. He led Vanessa to the palace, and the very next day announced that they were to be married. The wedding ship was to depart at sunset.

Ariel and her friends watched in despair as the sun lowered in the sky.

By chance, Scuttle discovered that Vanessa was really Ursula in disguise, and he called on all the sea creatures to stop the wedding. Sebastian went to find the Sea-King, and Flounder helped Ariel towards the wedding ship.

Suddenly birds swooped down on Vanessa. A lobster pinched her nose and some seals flipped her into the wedding cake!

In the chaos, Vanessa's seashell necklace broke and the beautiful voice inside flew back to its rightful owner. Eric, released from the spell, took Ariel in his arms. Just as he was about to kiss her, the sun set below the horizon.

Straightaway Ariel was turned back into a mermaid. Ursula grabbed her and dived into the water. Her evil cackle echoed eerily round the ship.

"Ursula, stop!" thundered King Triton, rearing up in front of the Sea-Witch. "Let her go!"

"No!" cried Ursula. "She's mine now. You see we made a deal! However, I might be willing to make an exchange for someone even better," she suggested slyly.

Triton felt he had no choice. He changed the signature on the scroll to his own and handed over his magic trident to the Sea-Witch.

I hereby grant unto URSULA the Witch of the Sea... one voice,

for all eternity
signed
TRITON

"At last! It's all mine," Ursula screamed.
"I am the ruler of the ocean!" Just then a
sharp pain shot through her arm. It was a
harpoon thrown by Eric. He had come to
rescue Ariel.

The Sea-Witch swelled with anger and towered above them. She summoned all the sea's power and stirred up a giant whirlpool, dragging up ancient shipwrecks from the seabed.

Eric scrambled on board one of the decks and, somehow, he reached the ship's steering wheel. Using all his might he aimed the broken bow directly at Ursula. And with a terrible scream she melted away into a pool of oil.

Triton's power was instantly restored. He rose to the surface and saw Ariel gazing lovingly at Eric, who was lying on the beach.

"She really does love him," Triton murmured to Sebastian. "I suppose the only problem left is how much I will miss her." Then with a flourish of his trident, the Sea-King granted Ariel her dearest wish – to be human for ever. Overjoyed, Eric and Ariel rushed into each other's arms.

A few later the couple were married, and all their friends were invited to the wedding. King Triton gladly gave Ariel and Eric his blessing, knowing they would live happily ever after.